DO YOU ENJOY BEI

WOULD YOU RATHER HAVE
NIGHTMARES
INSTEAD OF SWEET DREAMS?

ARE YOU HAPPY ONLY WHEN
SHAKING WITH FEAR?

CONGRATULATIONS ! ! ! !

YOU'VE MADE A WISE CHOICE.

THIS BOOK IS THE DOORWAY
TO ALL THAT MAY FRIGHTEN YOU.

GET READY FOR

COLD, CLAMMY SHIVERS

RUNNING UP AND DOWN YOUR SPINE!

NOW, OPEN THE DOOR—
IF YOU DARE !!!!

THE BEAST BENEATH
THE BOARDWALK

M. D. Spenser

Plantation, Florida

For Dierdre Killen

ISBN 1-57657-097-5
30621

EXCLUSIVE DISTRIBUTION BY PARADISE PRESS, INC.

Cover Design by George Paturzo
Cover Illustration by Eddie Roseboom

Printed in the U.S.A.

Chapter One

One minute, it was going to be the best summer vacation we ever had. In fact, it was going to be the best summer vacation we ever could have!

And then, not even a minute later, it turned into the worst summer vacation we ever had . . . or ever could have.

To be exact, it was going to be the worst summer vacation *I* could ever have.

I'll begin at the beginning.

My name is Alec Kelly. I'm twelve.

Near the end of last May, about ten days after my birthday, Mom and Dad called a family conference after dinner one night. They like to make a big thing out of sharing plans and stuff.

Dad said, "I have an announcement to make."

Sometimes when he says that, it's something

good. But not always.

"It's about our summer vacation this year," he said.

So it was going to be good, right?

"You know your mother and I like to discuss our plans with you, but this year things were a little complicated."

Oh, so now it was going to be bad!

The first part of what Dad said was fine. In fact, it was great!

Dad has an uncle named Louis — everybody calls him Louie — who owns an arcade on the boardwalk at Seacoast City in New Jersey.

I love Seacoast City! Everybody calls it Ess-Cee, for its initials.

It has a great beach, with beautiful, clean, white sand. Usually, the water is great, warm enough to swim in, not too much seaweed, and the waves are nice, too. Usually, they're just right — big enough to jump into but not big enough to flatten you like a pancake.

Seacoast City also has a great boardwalk. That's the part I like best. For about a mile on the boardwalk, there's nothing but games and rides and arcades and places to eat.

There's pizza and hot dogs and sausage heroes and custard and Belgian waffles and ice cream. There's every good kind of food you could possibly imagine.

I could spend the rest of my life there and never leave, not even for a day!

My uncle's arcade isn't the biggest one on the boardwalk, but it's terrific. It's called Lucky Louie's Arcade and it's filled with pinball machines and electronic games, and he always has all the newest ones.

He has some old-fashioned games, too, like skee-ball, and I really like the old ones. And he has those machines where you operate a hanging claw and try to lift a prize out of the bottom. I'm pretty good at those, though the prizes aren't always that great.

I like them all, really, but I think my favorites are the old pinball machines. I like the way the lights flash and the bells ring and the balls carom around inside the machine. The only thing I hate is when I get a little too excited and tilt the machine, and the lights go off, and I just have to stand there helplessly watching the ball dribble down and out of play.

But I'm pretty good. I don't tilt the machines very often. And I love to play.

I can spend hours in Lucky Louie's Arcade.

We used to go to Seacoast City for a couple of weekends each summer. We've been doing that for as long as I can remember. When we did that, we'd stay in a motel.

Last summer, we went to Seacoast City for a whole week. Mom and Dad rented a house. It was great. We could walk to the beach and to the boardwalk. At home, we'd usually have hamburgers and hot dogs and stuff like that for dinner.

Last year, Dad said that next year — that is, this year — I could for the first time go on the boardwalk and to the arcades by myself in the evenings.

And this year had finally come!

The big news Dad announced at the family conference was that this year we weren't going to spend a week in Seacoast City. This summer, we were going to spend a month! And Uncle Louie had said I could help out at the arcade if I wanted to.

If I wanted to? Of course I wanted to!

That was when I thought this was going to be the best summer vacation ever.

A month at the beach!

A month in the arcade!

Then Dad told us the rest of the news and the greatest summer anybody ever had suddenly turned into the opposite. By the time he was done, I was wishing I'd never even heard of Seacoast City!

Chapter Two

I was daydreaming about the games in the arcade. Dad was still talking. I suddenly realized he was talking about somebody I didn't know.

"Who?" I asked.

"Your cousin," Mom said. "Your cousin, Mary, from Galway in Ireland."

I couldn't believe what I was hearing.

"But she's in Ireland," I said. "On the other side of the Atlantic Ocean!"

I know that was a dumb thing to say. Of course, Ireland is on the other side of the Atlantic Ocean. Of course, all anybody in Ireland had to do was get on an airplane. Of course, I sounded like a dope. It's just that what I was hearing made me stupid.

"Alec, what's the matter with you?" my father asked.

"Nothing, Dad," I said. "Sorry."

"Of course, you probably don't remember her," Mom said. "You were both very little the last time they were here. But you know who she is."

"Right, Mom," I said. I knew as much as I needed to know, that was for sure.

"They live in Galway, Ireland," Dad said. "Mary is going to come here for a month in the summer, so she'll come to Seacoast City with us. We've made all the arrangements. It will be nice to have her visit America and come to the shore with us? Won't it, Alec?"

"Yeah," I said. "Nice."

"Alec," Dad said sharply. "What exactly is wrong with you?"

"Nothing, Dad," I said. "Sorry. I was just thinking about some other stuff."

"Well," Mom said, "we certainly hope that you'll do everything you can to make Mary feel welcome here. She's part of the family, you know. The last time she was in America, she was too young to know anything, but now she should really have a good time on this trip."

"Alec," Dad said, "we also talked with your aunt and uncle about something else."

He stopped talking and just looked at me in that serious way he has sometimes. This sounded to me like another big announcement.

"Oh?" I said. "What about?"

"Well, we thought that next year, maybe, you might like to spend a month with them in Ireland."

When I heard that, my heart stopped beating for a few seconds. I forgot to breathe. That was pretty exciting news. The trouble was that I wasn't sure if it was good news or bad news. I didn't know what to think about it.

"Gee, Dad," I said. "That's great."

"Hmm," he said. "You might show a little more interest."

"Next summer is so far away," I said. "I guess I'm more interested in this summer."

"Well, okay," Dad said. "We need to talk a little more about this summer, anyway."

"What do you mean, Dad?" I said.

Dad explained what he meant very carefully.

That's when I got the bad news.

Chapter Three

Now that I was twelve, he told me, he and Mom thought we could do some things differently. He said that one reason we could go away for a month was that I was older now. I was supposed to be more responsible.

They'd expect me to help out more than usual while we were away.

"No problem, Dad," I said.

I'd have to help with food shopping, too.

"No problem," I said.

And he assumed there wouldn't be any problem about my doing my share of keeping the house clean, too.

"No problem," I said again.

I meant it, too. I was willing to do my share of things in the family. It was something else that I was worried about, something I knew my parents

9

wouldn't understand.

"What about Mary?" I said.

"She'll have to help, too," Mom said.

"Oh, I know that," I said. "She'll be part of the family, so she'll have to do her share like everybody else. I was sort of wondering . . . what she's like."

"Oh," Mom said, smiling. "Alec, I'm sure you'll like her. Of course, I don't know her personally, any more than you do. I know that she's an excellent student. I know she gets very good grades in school."

Oh, no! I thought.

"Oh," I said. "That's nice."

"We'll expect you to be extra nice to her. You'll sort of be her host in America, you know. You can take her around in Seacoast City and show her things."

I'd rather die! I thought.

"Sure," I said. "That'll be great."

Dad was giving me a funny look. I knew I should drop this subject, but there was one thing I had to know.

"How old is she?" I asked, as casually as I could manage.

"Oh," Mom said, "she's your age. She's twelve."

That wasn't good enough. I had to know more.

"Oh," I said, "that's great. Say, uh . . . do you happen to know when her birthday is?"

"Her birthday?" Mom said. "It was just last month. The twentieth, right, Dan?"

"April twentieth," Dad said.

"Oh," I said, "that's great."

I was sounding like an echo of my own voice.

And I was smiling so much that every muscle in my face hurt.

So that was the end of the great summer. I had a girl cousin coming to stay with us for a month. And she was older than me. And a month counts for a lot when you're twelve. And I was supposed to be her "host."

Great.

What I didn't know then was that I'd actually be lucky to have my cousin there in Ess-Cee.

What I also didn't know then was that fate, or something, had planned a really horrible surprise for the summer.

I shiver every time I think about that horrible, disgusting thing . . .

It nearly killed both of us. And we would have died an ugly, messy death.

We were lucky. We were both there to keep each other alive!

Chapter Four

But of course, I knew none of that as our trip began. I was just looking forward to a nice, entertaining vacation.

Seacoast City was just a few miles ahead. Ess-Cee, here we come!

Mom and Dad always said I was just imagining it, but I knew I could smell the ocean as soon as we turned off the Garden State Parkway. The air was a little cooler, and kind of hazy white near the horizon, and the smell of salt and seaweed and whatever else goes into ocean water hit my nostrils.

When we turned off the exit ramp onto the local road that led to the beach was when I usually got really excited.

But I was trying to keep calm this time.

I was in the back seat of the car. Mary, my Irish cousin, was sitting on the other side in the back.

Mary didn't show any reaction at all as we rode along. She'd been looking out the window every minute since we'd left New York. She hardly said a word the whole time, nearly two hours.

Not that I really minded. But I thought it would be nice if she said a little something every now and then.

I looked over at her.

"We're almost there," I said.

"Oh," she said, "that's nice. It wasn't really such a long ride, was it?"

Oh, boy, I thought. This is going to be a long month!

"We'll be there in a few minutes," I said. "We just have to cross the bridge over the bay, and then we're there."

Mary glanced across at me for a second. "Good," she said. "I'm looking forward to it." Then she went back to looking out the window.

It was going to be a very long month!

I was looking out the window myself. I loved that road! Every inch of it brought us closer to Ess-Cee.

And then, at last, we were crossing the bridge. We turned to the right, to the left, then to the left again. We went down a few streets, getting closer to the beach every second.

Suddenly, Dad turned into a gravel driveway and stopped the car.

"Here we are!" he said. He sounded as happy as I felt.

The house was less than a block from the beach and the boardwalk. On the boardwalk, right at the end of our block, was my uncle's arcade. I could see the big red neon sign flashing on and off above it: LUCKY LOUIE'S ARCADE.

We were going to live in the house, but that arcade was going to be my real home for the next month.

It's just a good thing that I couldn't see what was waiting under the boardwalk and the arcade.

If I had, I never would have gotten out of the car!

Chapter Five

I helped Mom and Dad unpack the car. Mary helped too. She was pretty strong for a girl.

I worked fast, hauling suitcases and boxes up the driveway and into the living room. I wanted the vacation to begin already. I wanted to check out the arcade, to see if perhaps Uncle Louie had bought any new games.

The house was okay, I guess. It had a gigantic living room and a dining area and a kitchen and a laundry room downstairs. Upstairs, there were four small bedrooms.

It was just a house.

Mom and Dad acted like it was a castle or something.

"Yeah, wow, it looks terrific," I said.

I glanced at the pile of stuff we'd brought inside.

"I guess that's everything, right, Dad?"

"Well," Dad said, "it's everything we brought. And I think we brought everything we own. I just hope there's room for all this stuff."

I was dying to get out of there. Mom came to the rescue.

"Dan," she said, "I think you and I should get all this stuff put away. Then we have to go to the supermarket. I think Alec and Mary should take their bags up to their rooms. Then they can go and see Uncle Louie for a little while. How does that sound?"

That sounded perfect to me. I was already grabbing my suitcase out of the pile and starting up the stairs.

Mom said Mary and I could go to see Uncle Louie at the arcade and take a walk on the boardwalk for an hour. Then we had to be back to go to the supermarket.

I hauled my bag upstairs. Mary did the same.

In about ten seconds, we were both hurrying along the sidewalk toward the arcade.

I hardly noticed the weather. The sky was

gray and there were some dark, nasty-looking clouds in the sky. They were moving fast, too, the way they usually do before a storm.

When I thought about it later, I realized that the weather when we arrived was the start of the bad things that happened.

But I wasn't concerned at the time. Storms can be fun sometimes.

And sometimes, a storm can be a bad one. And sometimes, you're right beside the ocean when it comes. And sometimes, as I was to learn, the storm stirs up some dead things that are supposed to stay dead.

When that happens, a storm is no fun at all.

That particular storm already had plans for Mary and me. Big plans.

Chapter Six

It was exactly one o'clock when Mary and I left the house.

The next hour went by in a flash. In fact, the whole afternoon went by in a flash.

As things turned out, the next couple of days went by in a flash. I just wish they'd gone by in a blur, because then I wouldn't be haunted by the things I saw in those days and nights. But I wasn't that lucky. I remember it all too clearly.

Things started to get weird that very first afternoon.

At first, though, everything was great.

I took Mary to the arcade to meet Uncle Louie.

I always liked Uncle Louie. I would have liked him even if he didn't own an arcade on the boardwalk. And even if he weren't my uncle.

He gave us a big welcome and said how happy he was to see Mary and how he could hardly believe how big she'd gotten. You know, all the usual stuff. He asked about her parents in Ireland. He was happy to hear that they were fine.

It went on and on for a while. Mary was perfectly polite, and my uncle said she was charming. He also said her Irish accent was charming.

I had to say I thought it was charming, too.

All I wanted to do was see what new games he had. And I wanted to see some of the old ones and maybe play a few before we had to go home.

All around us, the lights on the games were flashing. Buzzers and horns and sirens and music and electronic voices were coming out of all the games. There were glass cases all around the walls. They were filled with prizes you could get by saving up points you won in the games.

Outside on the boardwalk and inside the arcade, too, you could smell food, especially popcorn and hot dogs. They made my mouth water.

The place was packed with kids and young people. Everybody wore shorts or bathing suits, and lots of people wore dumb-looking hats to keep the sun off their heads, though there wasn't any sun just at the moment. Only ominous dark clouds.

Everybody was laughing and having a good time.

"It's busy this afternoon," Mary said.

Uncle Louie said, "Well, I hate to say it, because everybody hates bad weather at the beach. But when the weather isn't so nice for sunbathing and swimming, people come to the boardwalk. And a lot of them come to Lucky Louie's Arcade!"

He laughed. Mary laughed along with him. It was easy to see why everybody liked her so much.

"Alec," Uncle Louie said, "you're going to find a lot of changes in the arcade."

"You got a lot of new games?" I asked.

"Oh, we have a lot of new games. More than usual, this year. You'll have to try them all out and tell me which ones you like. I need your professional opinion."

"Sure!" I said.

"You may not like all the changes, though. I know how much you love the old games and the old pinball machines. But not everybody likes the old ones as much as you do."

"What do you mean?"

"I've had to take most of the old games out of the arcade. I still have them, though."

I loved those old games, especially the old pinball machines. They were like old friends.

"What did you do with them?"

"They're still here," Uncle Louie said. "I dug out some of the sand underneath the arcade and built a storeroom. They're down there. Do you want to take a look?"

"Sure!" I said.

Uncle Louie reached under the counter. He handed me a roll of quarters wrapped in paper and told me to use them in the machines. He pointed to a trap door in the floor behind the counter.

"Be careful going down the steps," he said. "And watch your head."

"I'll come too," Mary said behind me.

I'd completely forgotten about her.

I pulled the trap door open. The wooden steps and the room below were dark. As I started down, Uncle Louie switched on the light from upstairs.

"There's an extension cord for electricity," he said. "Just plug in whichever games you want to play."

All my favorite old games were down there. Most of them were old pinball machines, the kind that had wooden legs and frames around the glass.

The storeroom was under the arcade and stretched far enough to go partly under the boardwalk toward the ocean.

Uncle Louie closed the trap door above us.

And that was exactly when the bad stuff started to happen for real.

Chapter Seven

I must have been looking around at all the old games. I know I certainly wasn't watching where I was going.

I tripped on the last step and went flying. Behind me, Mary made some sort of choking sound.

With a thud, I landed flat on my face on the floor. For a second, I was stunned. Then I smelled the fresh wood smell of the floor. I realized my lip was cut and blood was running down my chin.

I felt Mary's hands on my shoulders. She was helping me to sit up. I sat up and started breathing again.

Mary was fishing for something in the pocket of her jeans.

"Here!" she said. "Take this. Your lip is bleeding. Go ahead! Use the tissue!"

How come girls always happen to have so

much stuff handy just when you need it? And how come there's always a girl around when you make a fool of yourself? I must have really looked stupid, falling on my face like that.

Mary must have been reading my mind.

"It's all right," she said. "Anyone could have taken a fall like that. Here, your lip is still bleeding a bit."

She took the tissue from me, folded it over, and dabbed at my lip. I felt so stupid, I didn't even turn away or tell her to stop.

"There," she said. "I think it's stopped bleeding now. And I've wiped the blood off your chin."

"Oh, no!" I said.

When I fell, the roll of quarters must have flown out of my hand. There were bright, shiny quarters all over the floor, all the way to the other end of the storeroom and under all the game machines.

I took a deep breath and pulled myself together.

"Uh, thanks," I said quietly. "I mean, thanks

for having a tissue."

Mary stuffed the tissue back in the pocket of her jeans, blood and all.

"Well, let's get on with it," she said. "We have to pick up all these coins."

"Quarters," I snapped. I was trying to teach her to understand American money, and I guess I was none too patient about it.

"Yes, that's right, quarters," she said. "I'll remember now."

She was already crawling around on her hands and knees, picking them up. I went to work at the other end of the room.

A roll of quarters is ten dollars. That's forty quarters. We found thirty-seven. When we gave up looking for the last three, I went and sat on the steps. Mary came and sat beside me.

All of a sudden, she hit me with a question I wasn't expecting.

"Why don't you like me?" she said.

I was stunned. I didn't know what to answer.

"You don't like me, I know it," she said.

"I don't *not* like you," I said.

That sounded dumb.

"I do like you."

That didn't sound right either.

"We might just as well like each other and learn to get on together," she said. "After all, we're stuck with each other, aren't we?"

I shrugged. Her accent sounded funny, but I was sort of getting to like it.

"Well," she said, "you can be horrible to me and we'll both have a terrible time. Or you can be nice and we'll both have a good time."

I hate it when a girl makes perfect sense.

"Okay," I said. "I'd rather be friends."

"Fine, then," she said. "We'll be friends."

We shook hands.

Maybe it happened because we were both a little embarrassed, or because the tension was over. Whatever the reason, at the same moment, we both burst out laughing.

It was the last time either one of us laughed for a long, long time.

Chapter Eight

We used a few of the quarters to play games, but my mind was really on other things.

I'd fallen down the stairs. I'd lost some of the money Uncle Louie had given us. I'd cut my lip and Mary had to help me with the bleeding. I'd made an idiot of myself in front of her. And she'd been nicer than I was.

So far, this vacation was not starting out so great.

And I'd dripped blood on the floor and it had stained the wood. I noticed it as I turned away from one of the pinball machines.

Mary noticed and looked where I was looking.

"We can take care of that," she said.

"How?" I said.

Oh boy, I was sounding dumber every time I

opened my mouth.

"Your uncle must have used some sandpaper when he built these steps," she said. "We'll find it and use it to scrape off the stain."

"Good idea," I mumbled.

Why hadn't I thought of that?

Then she looked me straight in the eyes.

"No one has to know you fell down the steps."

Suddenly, I realized what she was doing. She was offering me a sign of friendship, a secret we had together. Besides, if my parents knew I'd fallen down the stairs, there'd be a lot of fuss and bother.

"Okay," I said.

It wasn't much, but she accepted it. We had agreed to be friends.

Suddenly, Mary shivered.

"It's quite damp down here, isn't it?" she said.

And suddenly, I shivered myself.

It was summer and the weather was hot. When we'd walked to the arcade from the house, the sky had been dark and cloudy, and maybe the temperature outside had been a little cooler than usual for summer.

Here in the storeroom under the arcade and under the boardwalk, though, it was actually chilly. I hadn't noticed before because I was so distracted, but it was definitely damp and chilly down here. I shivered again.

Mary was hugging herself to keep warm.

"Alec, really, I'm cold here," she said. "And, besides, I'd like to go up and see the rest of the arcade before we have to go home."

"Sure," I said. "Let's go."

The truth is, I thought that if I stayed in that storeroom a minute longer myself, I'd be shivering like I had the plague or something. I didn't know what was wrong, besides the chill and the dampness, but I knew I suddenly wanted to get out of there.

I went up the stairs first and pushed open the trap door. I held it open while Mary came up.

The last thing I saw down there before closing the trap door and switching off the light was my own blood on the floor of the storeroom under the boardwalk.

Outside, it had started to rain.

Chapter Nine

Uncle Louie was standing in the wide doorway of the arcade, looking out at the boardwalk. Rain was starting to spatter the weathered boards. Tourists were scurrying around, casting worried glances at the sky and looking for cover.

"Yep," Uncle Louie said, "it's going to be a bad one."

"A bad one?" I said. "What do you mean?"

"Hurricane," Uncle Louie said. "It's been moving up the coast all week. Don't you watch the news on television?"

"Not much, I guess," I said.

"A hurricane?" Mary said. "I've never seen a hurricane! That will be just brilliant!"

"Brilliant?" I said.

"Brilliant," Mary said. "It means great."

"Well," Uncle Louie said, "to tell you the

truth, I don't think it'll be either brilliant or great. A hurricane can do terrible damage. It can wash the beach away and maybe damage the boardwalk, or maybe rip up my arcade and cost me a lot of money. And if it's a really bad one, it can do worse than that."

"Like what?" Mary asked.

Uncle Louie looked very serious.

"One time," he said, "quite a few years ago, there was a terrible one. The winds drove the ocean all the way up the beach, right into the streets. The whole boardwalk was under water."

"Under water?" I said. "Right here?"

"Right here," Uncle Louie said. "In fact, it was worse than that. You know, we're on a peninsula here, and it's only about eight blocks wide."

Suddenly, I could see what happened.

"The bay is on the other side," I said.

"That's right. Naturally, the water level in the bay rose too. They met in the middle."

His words hung in the air for a second.

"You mean everything was under water?" Mary asked. "Everything?"

"Everything," Uncle Louie said. "All of Seacoast City was under about three feet of water."

"Three feet of water," Mary said quietly. "The houses, the cars . . ."

Her voice sort of just trailed away.

"And then there's the wind," Uncle Louie said. "A hurricane is really just a big wind. That one took the roofs off a lot of houses. It did a lot of damage on the boardwalk, too. Everything here is built of wood, you know. And there are all these big glass windows."

I was thinking of something else.

"And the people," I said.

"Seven people died in that storm," Uncle Louie said.

While we thought about that, the three of us turned to look out at the boardwalk again. There were a lot fewer people around than there had been before. And there was nobody on the beach.

Was it just my imagination, or was it really raining harder now than it had been?

Chapter Ten

"Lou!"

That was my father's voice. The three of us turned around and saw my father and mother. They had come into the arcade through the street door at the back.

They were both wearing yellow slickers that were wet from the rain. Dad was holding a dripping umbrella. Mom was holding two more yellow slickers with hoods.

Both of them looked pretty bedraggled. They had gotten wet in spite of the umbrella, and their hair was plastered to their heads.

Mom and Dad and Uncle Louie talked for a few minutes. It was all the usual stuff, about the family and how great everybody looked. I didn't think Mom and Dad looked so great, as wet as they were, and I thought Uncle Louie looked older than he used to, but I guess those weren't the polite things to say.

While they were talking, Uncle Louie kept glancing out at the boardwalk. The rain was hitting the wooden boards and bouncing when it hit. I thought Uncle Louie looked more worried every second.

"What's the latest on the radio about the storm?" he asked my father.

"It's not good," my father said. "Not good at all. Now they're saying it's moving faster than they thought it would. And it has turned sharply to the west. They were saying this morning that it was just going to brush the coast, and there was no cause for concern. But now it looks like it's headed our way."

"Are they saying when they think it will hit here?"

My father nodded. "They're predicting it will strike the coast between eight and ten tonight."

"Well, there goes most of a day's business," Uncle Louie said.

He looked out at the boardwalk and the rain again. Then he turned and looked around the arcade.

We all turned and looked.

There was hardly anybody left. There were the four teenage boys who worked for Uncle Louie. Their job was making change and getting the game machines running when they got stuck or something.

At the back door, the one that faced the street, there were three older kids. They kept trying to push each other out into the rain. I guess they were ready to leave, but nobody wanted to be the first one to step out into the downpour.

Besides them, I counted seven other people. And five of them were standing near us, watching the rain. Nobody was spending any money.

Uncle Louie sighed.

"It doesn't look like it's worth staying open," he said.

"Is there anything we can do?" Dad asked.

"Thanks, no," my uncle said. "I think I'll just check with some other merchants on the boardwalk. I'll see if they're going to close up early. I think I probably should. I worry about the glass doors when there's a strong wind."

Then two things happened all at once that

settled everybody's plans right away. A sudden gust of wind came along and a garbage can in the middle of the boardwalk blew over with a crash.

A second later, a man came dashing in from the rain. It turned out that he owned another arcade on the boardwalk about a block away. He wanted to know if Uncle Louie was going to stay open. They talked about the storm for a minute with my father. It was obvious what they should do. They decided to close.

The other man dashed back onto the boardwalk toward his own arcade.

"It's a lucky thing I have steel shutters to protect the doors," Uncle Louie said.

He called over his four employees and told them he was going to close up. He said they didn't have to bother with the usual routines. They could just leave their supply of coins under the counter and they'd all sort it out tomorrow.

Suddenly, everybody felt very worried about the storm. They were all in a hurry to do what they had to do. My father turned to Mary and me.

"I think you two better just go back to the

house. Stay there till your mother and I get back."

"Aren't we going with you?" I asked.

"No," Dad said. "We're just going to go across the bridge to the nearest supermarket and get some basic things. Water, food, that sort of thing. We might have to stay in the house a while."

"And batteries," Mom said. "And a little portable radio. Just in case."

Mom looked really worried. And she sounded worried, too. Which kind of made me worried, as well.

"Oh," she said, "here. I almost forgot. I bought these for both of you the other day. They'll come in handy."

She handed Mary and me the slickers.

Dad said, "The problem is that we also have to go to the telephone office. We have to give them a deposit to turn on the phone at the house."

"Take this, too," Mom said. "It's the key to the house. And, whatever you do, don't lose it. The rental office only gave us one. We'll get more made tomorrow."

The key was on a little chain with a blue

plastic thing that had the address written on it.

Uncle Louie had come back to join us.

"Speaking of keys," he said to my father, "you better take these. They're extras. This one opens all the padlocks on the steel shutters. This other one opens the locks on the doors. In case I can't get back here over the bridge in the morning, you can check on the place for me."

"Sure," Dad said. "But, you know, I think Alec better just take them back to the house now."

He handed me the keys. One had a red plastic thing on the chain. The other had a white thing. They both said "Lucky Louie's Arcade." I put them in my pocket with the house key.

Then, in about a minute, everybody disappeared. The arcade was closed and we were all outside. Mary and I stood back against the steel shutters, out of the rain.

Mom and Dad got into the car and drove off. Uncle Louie ran to the parking lot across the street.

We saw him jump into his car and speed off after
Mom and Dad, heading toward the bridge.

    And that was it. Mary and I were alone.

    And we were doomed.

Chapter Eleven

What a disaster! What a total disaster!

There was a television in the living room of the house that must have been made in prehistoric times. It was probably made before there even was such a thing as television. The picture was all zig-zaggy. Everything was green. And the volume was either very, very low or very, very loud.

We tried watching it for a while. In the first place, there was nothing good on. In the second place, we could hardly even tell what was on.

I checked the kitchen. There was nothing to eat or drink. Absolutely nothing.

And it was cold. And the windows were all rattling because the wind had gotten stronger. And there was a little pane of glass missing from the window in the kitchen. The wind came howling in through the opening. That made the house even colder.

I thought about bringing my boom box downstairs. I had brought about a dozen CDs with me, and I figured we could listen to some of them. I went upstairs to my room. I was looking through the CDs when I decided I didn't feel like doing that.

I went downstairs.

Mary was looking through the cabinets in the kitchen. She had already put on a sweater.

It was getting colder in the house by the minute. I went up to my room and got out a sweater and put it on.

Great! I thought. We come to Seacoast City in the summer and I have to put on a sweater the very first day.

And I was bored. I went downstairs.

"Look!" Mary said from the kitchen. "You missed this. There was a box in the cabinet here. It has seven tea bags. I'll make tea."

"Tea?" I said.

"Yes. That's what we do at home. Whenever something goes wrong or the weather is especially terrible, we make a pot of tea. I've put the water on."

"There's no milk," I said.

Mary shrugged. "We'll drink it black."

I hate tea without milk. Everything was just a total disaster. I went to one of the front windows and looked out.

It wasn't even two-thirty in the afternoon, but outside it was nearly as dark as evening. Some papers and a plastic soda cup and a popcorn bucket blew past on the sidewalk. A gigantic puddle was forming on the gravel in the driveway.

And I was starving.

I looked out the window for a while.

Behind me, Mary said brightly, "Tea is ready. We can have it in the living room while we watch television."

As I said, it was a total disaster!

Chapter Twelve

Then I had a great idea! I started digging in my pockets.

"How much money do you have?"

Mary's face broke into a grin.

"Brilliant!" she said.

She pulled out one of those little wallets girls carry. I already had my wallet out. I counted. I had eight dollars. Plus I had all the quarters we hadn't used in the storeroom at the arcade. I spilled them out on the coffee table in front of the sofa.

I counted quickly. The quarters added up to six dollars and fifty cents. I also had five dimes of my own. That made seven dollars. And with the eight in my wallet, that made a total of fifteen dollars.

"Fifteen dollars!" I announced triumphantly.

"I have thirty pounds," Mary said.

"What?"

"Thirty pounds," she said. "That's Irish money. I think it's about fifty dollars in American money."

"Too bad we're not in Ireland," I said.

Mary gave me one of those looks.

"And," she said, "I have twenty American dollars."

"Twenty dollars!"

"Your mother gave it to me last night." She held up the bill. "She didn't want me to be penniless in America, she said."

I wasn't even jealous.

"We have thirty-five dollars!" I said. "Let's go get some food!"

"Good thinking!" Mary said.

We gathered up the money from the table. Then we grabbed our slickers and pulled them on.

We were at the door when Mary said, "Where should we go? Do you think the shops will be open?"

I hesitated for a second, thinking fast.

"We could go up to the main street," I said, "but I don't know what kind of stores there are around here. Or we could go up to the boardwalk. We could get hamburgers or pizza or something like that."

Hot food sounded like a good idea just then, since it was getting so cold out.

"But won't everything on the boardwalk be closed?" Mary said.

"There are three or four places to eat in every block on the boardwalk," I said. "They can't all be closed."

"All right, then," Mary said. "Let's go!"

I opened the door and we stepped outside into the rain. We had to turn away from the wind. It was blowing so hard that it took our breath away.

I locked the door and put the key in my pocket. My feet felt wet and ice cold. We were standing in a puddle.

"Come on!" I yelled.

We started off toward the boardwalk, running and splashing through the rain.

It was my fault. I was the one who made the decision to go to the boardwalk instead of the stores.

It wasn't my fault that there was a . . . *thing* under the boardwalk.

But it was definitely my fault that we walked right in to meet it!

Chapter Thirteen

We ran up to the boardwalk and stopped in front of the door to Uncle Louie's Arcade. I looked right and left. I could see signs swinging in the wind. Some of them were still turned on and flashing. But I couldn't see any food place that looked like it was open.

A couple of people ran past us on the board-walk, their hands on their heads to keep their hats from blowing off in the wind. There were three or four other people in sight, far away. They looked like they were running too.

"Come on!" I said. "There has to be a place along here."

Three long, wet blocks later, we found a pizza place that was just closing. We dashed inside.

"Can we get some pizza?" I said.

The man looked at me like I was crazy.

"You want a whole pie?" he said. "Here. I'll give you this whole pie. It's still warm. Give me five dollars."

It was a good deal.

"Sure," I said.

I pulled the five-dollar bill out of my wallet and put it on the counter. In a few seconds, the man had put the pizza in a box and tied up the box with string. I lifted it off the counter.

"Where are we going to eat it?" Mary asked me as we turned toward the doorway of the pizza shop.

I had another of my great ideas.

"The arcade!" I said. "And we can get sodas out of the machines there."

"Brilliant!" Mary said.

It was my bright idea again.

And so it was my fault that we were doomed.

Chapter Fourteen

We ran back up the boardwalk to the arcade.

The rain was really coming down. Worse than that, the wind was howling. Every sign on the boardwalk was swinging wildly. Garbage cans were rolling along, pushed by the wind.

When we got to the arcade, the wind was blowing so hard that the steel shutters on the doors were rattling. Even the wood of the boardwalk sounded like it was groaning beneath our feet.

Mary held the pizza while I got out the keys.

"Please hurry!" she said. "I'm freezing!"

I was, too. My hands were so cold and wet that I could hardly handle the keys. It took me a minute or two but I finally got the padlock open and pushed the shutter up enough to get at the lock on the door.

Then I got that open and pushed the door in,

and then we were inside.

It was pitch black.

"Stay here!" I said.

I felt my way to the left, trying to remember where everything was in the arcade. I forgot that everything was different from last year. And when we had been here earlier, we had spent most of our time downstairs.

Finally, I found the counter, then the wall. I slid one hand along it and moved slowly forward. At last, my fingers touched a panel of electric switches. There must have been twenty of them. I pushed the first three switches my fingers touched.

Lights came on.

And so did a horrible laughing sound that was really the cackling of a witch!

Ha ha! Hee tree tree! Ha ha! Hee tree tree!

A shiver went up my spine. It felt as if I'd been touched by an icy fingernail.

Chapter Fifteen

Mary screamed!

She had just been crouching to squeeze under the steel shutters and through the doorway. That horrible, cackling laugh made her jump as she was halfway through.

Ha ha! Hee tree tree! Ha ha! Hee tree tree!

What was it? Where was it coming from?

"Alec! Alec! What is it?"

I heard the panic in Mary's voice. Actually, it was more like terror than panic. And I wasn't feeling so great myself.

All of this happened in maybe two or three seconds, but it seemed like it went on forever. My head snapped around. My eyes flew in every direction. I had to remind myself to take a breath.

Ha ha! Hee tree tree! Ha ha! Hee tree tree!

There it was! Boy, did I feel stupid!

"It's okay!" I called out to Mary. She was standing with her back pressed to the door.

"What . . . What is it?"

The hideous laughter was still going on, cackling like a witch in the mountains in the middle of the night. Now that I was breathing again, I could feel my heart hammering madly in my chest.

"It's okay!" I yelled to Mary. "It's over here. Come and look."

"Where?" she called.

"Right here."

About fifteen feet from where I was standing was a really old fortune-telling machine. Inside its glass case there was a horrible-looking witch. She was wearing a black robe and she had a pointed hat on her head.

It was only a doll, no more than three feet high, and she was sitting in a little chair. There were glass eyes in her hideous face and they glittered in the light. Her head moved slowly from side to side. Every few seconds, those glass eyes caught the light and flashed, as if the light was inside her. She seemed to be looking right at me.

Ha ha! Hee tree tree! Ha ha! Hee tree tree!

Mary had come up beside me. She touched me on the arm. I jumped right out of my skin!

"Yeow!" I yelled.

Goose flesh crept up my neck and down my arms.

"Alec, make it stop! Please! Make it stop!"

I could hardly breathe, as if I'd just run ten blocks without stopping.

Ha ha! Hee tree tree! Ha ha! Hee tree tree!

"Alec, please!"

"Okay, okay!" I said quickly.

I bent down and looked for the electric cord. There it was. It went into a heavy-duty socket in the floor where other machines were plugged in. I pulled the plug out.

Silence! At last!

"Oh, Alec," Mary said softly.

"Yeah!" I said. "Yeah!"

"Oh, I'm so glad that stopped. That horrible laughter. I'm still shivering!"

"It's okay now," I said. "Just listen to all that beautiful silence."

Well, the laughter had stopped. And my heart had slowed down. And I was breathing again.

But there was no silence.

What I heard now was even worse than that horrible, cackling laugh. Together, Mary and I turned toward the door.

And the goose flesh crawled up the back of my neck again.

Chapter Sixteen

When the witch's laughter made Mary jump, she had just let the front door close by itself. It wasn't locked.

On the outside, the steel shutter was raised about four feet high. The wind was blowing the door, and the door kept banging with a loud thud every couple of seconds.

Even though the steel shutters were heavy, they were being pounded mercilessly by the wind. Now they were rattling in their tracks as if the devil himself were trying to tear them away from the door.

"I better lock that door!" I said.

I started toward the door.

"I'm coming with you!" Mary said.

She stayed right behind me. I could feel her hand on my shoulder. Just as I got to the door, there was a tremendous crash of metal against the metal of the shutters. It sounded like a bomb.

We both jumped back about three feet.

"What was that?"

"I . . . I better go outside and see," I said.

Believe me, it was a lot easier to say that than to do it. "Outside" was just about the last place in the world I wanted to be right then.

"Be careful!" Mary breathed behind me.

I was at the door. It was still banging and thumping as the wind pushed against it.

"Here," I said to Mary. "You hold the door open. I'll crawl under the shutter."

"Be careful!" she said again.

"I will," I said. That was exactly what I intended.

"I'll just take a quick look around, up and down the boardwalk."

"Don't go all the way out on the boardwalk!"

"I need to see if it's safe to go home," I said. "I'll just stick my head out and take a quick look."

Do you know the expression, "Famous last words?" Those were my famous last words.

Mary pulled the door open. I got down on

my hands and knees and crawled out through the doorway, under the steel shutters.

My hands touched the cold, wet wood of the boardwalk.

I looked to my left. I saw part of a sign lying on the boardwalk. That must have been what hit the shutters and made that banging noise.

Farther along the boardwalk, I couldn't believe the sight I saw.

I looked straight ahead toward the beach. I couldn't believe what I saw there, either.

It was . . .

Then, in no more than about a tenth of a second, several things all happened at once.

I heard a deafening crash. I saw a flash of blinding light that seemed to go off inside my skull. I felt a dull, painful *whack!* right on the top of my head.

From far, far away, I heard a girl's voice calling my name.

Then I didn't hear or see or feel anything.

Chapter Seventeen

"Alec! Alec!"

"Ohhhhhh . . ."

I could hear myself groaning. I didn't want to groan, but I couldn't help it. It just came out of me, long and low and anguished.

"Alec, can you hear me?"

What I could hear best was the blood rushing in my ears. What I could feel best was the painful pounding in my head. And what I could see best was . . . Mary.

And right beside her, sort of overlapping her, there was another Mary.

I shook my head. That was a mistake! I groaned again.

Then slowly, slowly my head started to clear. I managed to sit up. Mary helped me sit back against the counter.

Then she left me for a few seconds. She came back with a roll of paper towels. She tore one off. Very gently, she began dabbing at my head.

That's when I realized that my hair and my face were wet with rain. And something else. I raised my hand to the side of my head.

Mary said sharply, "Don't!"

I lowered my hand and looked at it.

There was bright, red blood on my fingers.

Okay, here's what happened.

Just as I was looking around, with my head outside in the rain and the wind, a gigantic neon sign from the stand next to the arcade came crashing down to the boardwalk. It must have been swinging and swinging in the wind. Finally, the wind tore it loose.

My timing was perfect. The corner of it hit me right on the head.

When I got over the shock, I realized I had almost been killed.

Just the corner of the sign had hit me. That's what had cut my scalp and made it bleed. The force of it was enough to knock me out for a couple of seconds.

When Mary saw what had happened, she took hold of my ankles and dragged me back inside the arcade.

Once I could think clearly, I saw that her face was as pale as a ghost. Her eyes were wide and frightened.

But she was brave. She was still mopping up the blood in my hair. Two paper towels were now smeared red with my blood. There was blood on Mary's hands.

"Are you all right?" she said. I could hear her voice shaking with fright and worry.

"Yes," I said. "I'm okay. My head hurts, but I'm okay."

She told me about the crash of metal and glass that she thought had killed me. Then she said, "What did you see out there? What's it like outside?"

That question made my heart pound again.

And I definitely did not want to tell her what I'd seen outside.

Chapter Eighteen

"What did you see?" Mary asked again.

"You don't want to know," I said.

"What?" she demanded. She looked at me intently. "Tell me. I need to know."

"It looks . . ."

I hardly knew how to describe it.

"It looks like the end of the world," I said softly. "Or worse."

Mary stared at me. Her eyes were even wider open and more frightened than before.

Slowly, carefully, I tried to think of a way to describe what I'd seen. I opened my mouth. Then I hesitated. I could only think of one word to say.

"Monsters."

"Monsters?"

We could hear clearly what was happening outside. The wind was howling like a crazed beast. It pounded and thumped against the shutters, the doors, the walls.

All around us, inside the arcade, we heard the walls groaning as the wind pounded and pushed against them. The whole structure was built of wood. I hoped it was strong enough to stand up against a wind like that.

But I wasn't sure. And that scared me.

The wind was everywhere, howling and screaming and whistling. It was rattling and thumping just as hard against the shutters at the back of the arcade, which faced the street, as it was on the boardwalk side.

But that wasn't all.

The wind was pounding everything, the boardwalk and all the stands on it. It was hitting the rides a few blocks away. It was striking all the houses in Seacoast City.

It sounded as if it had only one intention, to flatten everything in its path. And if it couldn't flatten everything, it would just tear everything apart.

That's what I had seen when I looked outside at the boardwalk.

I'd seen something else, too. I was trying to remember what it was . . .

My head still hurt, my vision was blurry, and my memory was hazy. Oh, yes, now I remembered ...

Signs were hanging from the stands along the boardwalk. The wind had torn them loose. They were swinging wildly and banging against the walls they were attached to.

As I looked up the boardwalk to the left, I saw one break free from its building and come crashing down. Metal and glass shattered and flew in every direction.

And then the wind picked up all those little bits of metal and glass and wire. It lifted them from the boardwalk into the air. They swirled around, up and down, in a gigantic airborne whirlpool of sharp shards of glass and debris, as if they were trying to go in every direction at once.

And then they were whipped away and just went sailing through the air.

I saw a thin metal sign tear away from a wall just twenty feet away from where I was.

It was just a sign that had ice cream prices or

something like that on it. I guess it had been nailed to the wooden wall.

In about half a second, the corner of it started shaking. Then the corner bent up. Then the whole sign just flipped itself into the air.

It flew like a rocket right across the boardwalk.

It hit the back of a wooden bench that faced the beach. And one corner of the sign buried itself, like the point of an arrow, a couple of inches deep in the bench.

It was just sticking out of the bench and shivering in the wind. Then the wind tore it free and it sailed up and up and out of sight.

The wind was roaring like a wild animal and tearing madly at everything it touched.

Part of the wooden fence at the edge of the boardwalk, overlooking the beach, had been torn loose. I could see the splintered wood.

Some boards in the boardwalk itself had been pulled loose. I couldn't even guess how far away the wind had carried them by now.

Broken bits and pieces of things were flying

through the air every place I looked.

I tried to describe all of this to Mary. She just stared at me.

"The wind is like a monster," I said. "It's like one of those monsters in those Japanese movies. Something like Godzilla or Rodan. It's just throwing everything around and tearing everything to bits."

"We have to stay here," Mary said. "It's too dangerous to go outside."

"Right," I said.

"Something could come flying through the air and cut our heads off," she said quietly.

"Right," I said.

"We just have to wait here till it's over."

Then my head cleared and I remembered the other thing I'd seen. I shivered.

I didn't want to say this, but I had to.

"I'm not sure we can stay here very long."

"Why not?"

Then I had to tell her about the other thing I'd seen when I looked outside.

Chapter Nineteen

I took a deep breath.

"The ocean," I said.

Mary's hand flew up to her face. I didn't think her eyes could get any wider than they were already. But they did.

"It's up to the boardwalk," I told her. I tried to make my voice sound calm. "The waves were breaking at the edge of the boardwalk. They were pretty high, too."

"You mean they were breaking on the boardwalk?" She sounded awed by the thought.

"Well . . . yes," I said.

"Then we can't stay here!" she said. "The ocean will keep coming higher and higher. It will cross the boardwalk and the waves will break right here at the door!"

Mary said something else, but suddenly I

couldn't hear her. I couldn't hear anything. I couldn't talk, either.

The picture I had in my mind, the thing I'd seen, came into perfect focus.

I knew why I'd forgotten it. It was too horrible to remember. But I remembered it now, and now I had to think about it.

It was the thing I had seen in the waves breaking on the far side of the boardwalk. The thing I had seen in one of the waves in particular.

One gigantic wave, five or six times higher and bigger than the others, had crashed against the boardwalk. It foamed higher and higher in the air. It seemed to hang there for a fraction of a second before slamming down onto the boards.

And in that fraction of a second . . . I saw a face.

Chapter Twenty

"Alec, what's the matter with you?" Mary cried.

For a second, I couldn't answer her. I didn't know what to say.

Then I knew what I had to do. I had to keep quiet about what I'd seen. I couldn't tell her.

"Nothing," I said. "I guess my head just hurt me for a second."

"Well, don't frighten me like that!" she said.

"Sorry," I said. "I'm sorry."

What were we going to do? Suddenly, I had another of my great ideas.

"The back door!" I said.

I scrambled to my feet.

"If we have to, we can get out through the back door!"

"Alec . . ." Mary was saying.

"Come on!" I said. "Let's check it out!"

"Alec!"

Something in the way she was saying my name made me stop halfway across the arcade. I turned around and looked back at her. She was not following me. She stood stock still, and she looked at me, horrified.

"We can't go out that door," she said shakily.

I stared at her.

"The shutter on the door is locked from the outside. The padlock is outside."

She was right. We were trapped. Slowly, I walked back to where she was standing. I could tell that she was reading my mind. And I was reading hers.

After a few seconds, I said, "We should try to get out of here. Somehow. Some way. We've got to try."

Mary said nothing.

"If the water keeps rising," I said, "we'll have to get up higher."

Mary didn't say a word. She already knew what I still didn't want to admit, even to myself.

We were completely trapped.

Chapter Twenty-One

I suddenly felt exhausted.

I sat down on the floor and leaned back against the counter.

"Let me try and figure this out," I said. "There has to be a way out of this."

Mary sat down beside me.

Okay, I told myself. Think clearly. If the level of the ocean kept rising, we would have to get up higher. But the arcade had no second floor.

The only place to go higher here was the roof. And that certainly wasn't a good idea. It would be more than a little windy up there.

The house we were staying in had a second floor. Okay, we would have to get to the house.

How?

The back door of the arcade was closer to the house, but it was locked from the outside. So that was no good.

We could get out the front door onto the boardwalk, but that wasn't good, either. The wind was screaming like a maniac out there. Every few seconds, something banged into the walls of the arcade, something the wind was tossing around. Something that could kill us.

The proof was right there in the bloody paper towels on the floor.

Even if we did go out the front door, that would give us a very long route to the house. We would have to go along the front of the arcade on the boardwalk, up to the end of the block. Then we would have to go along the side of the arcade to the street behind it. Then we would have to cross the street and make our way down the block to the house.

And then I had an even worse thought.

I remembered Uncle Louie telling us how the level of the bay rose with the level of the ocean. I pictured the waters of the ocean and the bay meeting in the middle of Seacoast City.

I pictured waves hammering at cars and

houses. I pictured Mary and me pushing through all that water.

No way. We had to stay where we were.

Then suddenly I had another idea, about something completely different.

"What happened to that pizza?" I asked Mary.

For a second, she looked really surprised. She looked at me as if I was out of my mind. Then she turned and looked toward the door.

"I'll get it," she said.

I saw the box on the floor. All of a sudden, I was more hungry than tired. I was starving. And, for the moment, pizza seemed more important even than safety.

When Mary was first crouching and coming through the doorway, the cackling of the witch had made her jump. That's when she dropped the pizza box.

Do I have to tell you it landed upside down?

I turned it over and pulled the string off the box. The cardboard was soaked with rain. I opened the box.

What a mess!

There was cheese and sauce all over the inside of the box in one big, sticky glob. I started pulling it free from the wet cardboard.

"Take some," I said. "It's all we've got."

That was the wettest, coldest, soggiest, gummiest, stickiest, messiest, most horrible and disgusting pizza anybody ever ate in the history of the world.

We ate it. We ate every gooey bit of it. I knew it was our last meal on earth.

What a way to die.

Chapter Twenty-Two

We finished the pizza.

We sat in silence for a few minutes. Then, as if the two of us had been thinking exactly the same thing, we both stood up.

"We can't just sit here," Mary said. "We have to do something. We have to think of something."

That was obvious. The problem was, think of *what?*

Maybe the storm was dying down or the worst of it had passed us. But that wasn't thinking. It was hoping, and I knew that couldn't be true. I could hear the storm. It was still hurling things against the walls and rattling the doors. It was still screaming outside.

And, besides, I knew what was really out there.

"Maybe it's calmed down a little," I said. "I'll

go out and take a look."

"Alec, you can't go outside again. You nearly got killed the last time you went outside."

"I have to," I said. "It might be dying down."

There was nothing Mary could say to that. We went to the door. I looked at her. She pulled the door open. I dropped to my hands and knees, the way I had before.

Cautiously, I crawled forward and stuck my head out to look around. I wasn't afraid of the wind. I wasn't afraid of the things flying around in the air.

What I was afraid of was the face I had seen in the wave.

I raised my head. I made myself look straight across the boardwalk to where the waves were crashing against it. I made myself look to where I'd seen the face.

What I saw made my blood run cold.

Chapter Twenty-Three

The face was there.

But there was more. A huge wave came rolling and foaming toward the boardwalk. With a roar even louder than the wind, it crested, hung in the air for a second, then came crashing down on the wood.

In the second that it hung high in the air above the boardwalk, I saw the face.

It was an old man's face, a very old man's face. It was gray and white and blue and green, all the colors of the water.

It was a horrible face, twisted and distorted — human but, at the same time, not human at all. All around the face was long, streaming hair, green and blue and gray, flying in every direction.

The head tossed from side to side. The mouth was open wide. I felt that I could look right down that horrible throat.

That mouth was roaring. All the howling and screaming and screeching of the winds were coming out of that mouth. The wind itself was coming out of that mouth. The whole storm was coming out of that mouth.

And the eyes!

I saw them for only a second, only a fraction of a second. But I will never forget them. They were white and dark at the same time. They were shining with a terrible expression. They were the eyes of a maniac.

And they were looking right at me!

I shivered.

I stared at it. I couldn't move my eyes away from that face. And I couldn't close my eyes, either. It was as if that face made me look at it.

Those eyes showed me exactly what was behind them. They showed me exactly what the . . . *thing* was thinking.

I didn't know if it was a devil or a spirit or what. But I knew exactly what it was thinking.

It hated me. And it wanted me to know it. I

just stared.

I couldn't move.

It was only a fraction of a second, but it seemed to last forever.

That face tossed and turned. The mouth roared and foamed. The eyes flashed and glared at me, distorted by a hideous anger, misshapen by a horrible hatred.

But that wasn't even the worst of it.

Chapter Twenty-Four

It had arms. It had hands. And they were reaching out for me.

The face disappeared when the wave crested and crashed onto the boardwalk. But that was when I saw something I hadn't seen before.

The water splashed and foamed onto the wooden boards of the boardwalk. It spread out across the boards. I could see it even through the sheets of rain that slanted fiercely toward the ground.

The wave foamed across the boardwalk right toward me. For a second, it looked like a foaming pool of water sliding along, like any wave after it breaks and washes up the slope of a beach.

But this water broke up on the boardwalk. It divided.

First it looked like the wet and shiny tentacles of a gigantic octopus. Then it looked like arms. Dozens of arms, all reaching for me.

And then each of the separate streams that formed an arm divided again. Where it divided, fingers appeared.

Each finger seemed to have a dozen joints instead of just the two that a human finger has. Those fingers were twitching and grasping, clawing their way across the boardwalk.

They tore at the wood, dug into it, scraped and scratched at it.

They were all trying to get across the boardwalk. They were trying to reach me.

There were hundreds of them.

I wanted to close my eyes. I didn't want to see this. Even so, I knew I had to watch a little longer.

I had to wait for another wave to come. I don't know why, but I was unable to avert my eyes. It was as if I needed to see the thing that was going to do me in, to understand why I was going to die.

I needed to look my fate in the eye.

A series of waves crested and crashed against the boardwalk, but they were smaller than the one that had the face.

I waited. I knew it would come again.

And then I saw it.

This time it was laughing and roaring at the same time.

I shivered and kept on shivering. I tried to force myself to stop shivering but I couldn't. I wrapped my arms around myself for comfort, but still I shook like a leaf in the wind.

The face in the wave was thrown back, roaring with hideous laughter.

It crashed down.

The arms reached eagerly across the boardwalk. They stretched out, trying to reach me. Then the fingers sprouted from the arms. Hundreds of cold, wet fingers of foaming green water slithered toward me across the boardwalk.

Every bone and muscle and nerve in my body wanted to scramble backwards into the arcade and get away from those grasping fingers.

I forced myself to stay where I was.

I forced myself to wait.

There was something I was hoping with all my might that I would see.

And I saw it.

Chapter Twenty-Five

"Alec, come back in here!"

Mary was yelling and pulling at my legs, trying to get me back inside the arcade.

"Wait!" I yelled. "Wait a minute!"

"Come in here!"

"No!" I yelled over my shoulder. "There's something I need to see."

"If you don't come back inside, I'm coming out there with you!"

"Stay inside!" I shouted to her. "I'll come inside in a second."

"Look out!" Mary yelled.

"No!"

I was waiting for one more big wave. I wanted to see how far across the boardwalk those grasping fingers would reach.

And I wanted to see that horrible face once

more.

Maybe I was crazy. But I wanted to show it I wasn't afraid.

That was a lie, of course. I was very afraid. My knees felt weak, and my legs would barely hold me upright. My heart was thumping wildly in my chest.

I was terrified!

But I didn't want the *thing* to know that.

I was counting the waves. The ones that rolled in now, frothing and foaming, were smaller than the big one. They struck the far edge of the boardwalk and broke up with a fearsome crash, but they were nothing compared to the big one that was out to get me.

Another few seconds . . .

"Alec!"

"Wait!"

Here it was. I saw it coming. It was rising higher and higher as it rushed in toward the board-walk.

Behind me I felt a bump, a push. I was suddenly squeezed against the frame of the doorway.

The metal cut into my side.

The wave was building, rising up and up, gathering strength for its attack on the boardwalk.

"Alec, move!"

"No, Mary!" I shouted. "No! Don't come out here!"

The wave was curling to its topmost height.

"Alec, what's going on?" Mary shouted in my ear.

She was outside now, squeezed in the doorway under the half-closed shutter, on her hands and knees beside me.

The wave was about to break. The foam at the top of it was just starting to curl forward.

"Mary! Go back!"

"No!"

Too late!

The wave gathered itself into a towering wall of green and white water.

And there was the face. It tossed from side to side. The watery hair flew in every direction. The open mouth roared and the winds seemed to rush out of it. The eyes flashed with burning hatred.

Mary screamed.

Chapter Twenty-Six

The wave slammed down onto the board-walk.

This time, the boardwalk shook and trembled with the force of the blow. I felt the wood shuddering under my cold fingers.

The wind howled even louder than it had before. It was as if the thing was enraged because I had defied it. I had stayed there and stared it down.

I was shaking with fear, but I had done what I had to do. I had stayed there and faced it.

Now it was even angrier than before.

Its arms slithered and foamed across the boardwalk toward the arcade, toward me. Its fingers stretched and crawled and clawed at the wet wood. They slid and foamed, hundreds of them, reaching, reaching . . .

But they came no closer than they had the

two other times I had watched.

That was what I had needed to see.

Whatever that thing was, it was strong and wild and crazy, but it wasn't any stronger or wilder or crazier than it had been when I'd seen it before.

That didn't make me feel good, or better, but it certainly didn't make me feel worse. I had been afraid the thing would gather strength, growing stronger and stronger, and reaching further and further.

So far, that was not happening.

"Alec!"

Mary was still there, squeezed into the doorway beside me. I had hardly been able to think about her while I was watching for the thing.

Her voice was shaking. I realized that she'd seen the face in the wave.

Oh, no! I thought. That was exactly what should not have happened.

"Get back!" I told her. "Get back inside!"

"Alec! Alec, what was that?"

I didn't know how to tell her what she'd done. Of course, she hadn't done it carelessly or deliberately, but Mary had done the worst thing possible.

I had realized while I was out there that I had to stand up to that thing. I had to show it I wasn't afraid. And, somehow, I had.

That was why it hated me so much.

But now it had seen Mary. And it knew she was terrified.

And now it would come back again and again to show itself to her. It would boil and foam and crash. Its arms would rush across the wood.

And its fingers would be reaching for her.

Chapter Twenty-Seven

We were inside again.

In the excitement, we had both forgotten to pull our hoods over our heads. Our faces were wet with rain. Our hair was blown by the wind, soaking wet, and plastered oddly to our heads.

I wiped the water off my face and out of my eyes. Mary was staring at me. She couldn't move.

When she spoke, her voice sounded very tiny and very scared.

"Alec, what was that?"

She spoke so softly that I could barely hear her. I struggled to find the right words to answer her.

The real problem, of course, was that I didn't know the answer. All I knew for sure was that that thing was out there, in the waves and the wind.

And I knew it hated us. And I knew it wanted to get us. And when it got us, I knew what it would do to us.

If it got us.

I had to force myself to keep thinking like that. I had to think *if*, not *when*.

I couldn't allow myself to think like that. It would not get us. I wasn't going to let that happen. I had faced it once and I could face it again.

But I wasn't so sure about Mary.

She was pale and shivering. She didn't look like somebody who could go outside and deliberately face that thing again.

"Alec?" she said. "What are you thinking?"

I looked at her more carefully and then I realized something important.

After I had seen the face for the first time, I had been hit on the head by the sign and knocked unconscious.

If I hadn't been knocked unconscious, I would have looked exactly the way Mary looked now.

Maybe she could do it. I hoped she could do it.

She *had* to do it.

94

I took hold of her elbows. Her whole body was shaking. I looked right into her eyes.

"Mary, listen carefully to me," I said.

She nodded.

"We're going to be all right," I said. "I know we're going to be all right."

She just nodded again.

"But first," I said, "I have some really bad news for you."

__Chapter Twenty-Eight__

"What . . ?" Mary asked, her voice quavering. "What do you mean?"

I wished that Mary had not gone outside. And I wished I didn't have to tell her this. But I had no choice.

"Whatever that thing is out there, or whoever that thing is, it hates us. The second time I saw it, when I got a good look at it . . ."

"I know," Mary said. "I saw it. I saw the expression in its face."

She stopped and looked down. She took a deep breath.

"I saw its eyes," she said.

I waited a few seconds for her to stop shaking before I went on.

"Did you see what it looked like when the wave broke on the boardwalk?"

Mary nodded.

"It looked like snaky arms and hands and fingers," she said.

"Right," I said. "But there's something else I noticed."

There must have been a more hopeful sound in my voice when I said that. Mary looked up at me quickly.

"What was it?" she asked

"You only saw the wave with the face once," I said. "I saw it a few times." I quailed at the memory. "When it broke on the boardwalk, I watched to see how far the water — the fingers — reached."

I felt a little funny saying the rest of this. I wasn't bragging. That's not my style. And I had nothing to brag about, anyway. I had been terrified when I was out there.

But I'd had to do it, so I did.

"I looked right into those eyes," I said. "Right into them each time."

Mary shivered and hugged herself. She closed her eyes against the memory of that face, but it didn't seem to help. She shuddered even more.

"That thing roared louder each time," I said. "Its eyes looked more terrible each time, as if it was getting angrier and angrier. But it didn't come any closer."

"Are you sure?" she asked. There was pleading in her eyes.

"Yes," I said firmly. "I'm positive. I watched the exact same spot on the boardwalk each time. There was a broken board, so I could tell. It didn't come any closer."

"So that's sort of good, isn't it?" she asked.

"Yes and no," I said. "I think it didn't come any closer, or it *couldn't* come any closer, because it knew I wasn't afraid of it. At least, it thought I wasn't afraid of it."

"Well, that's good!" she said. She tried to look hopeful.

I knew how much Mary wanted to believe what she was saying. But she was wrong.

"Mary," I said, "it saw you. It knew *you* were afraid."

"Oh." Her face fell.

I let her think about that. It would be much

better if she figured out herself what she had to do. Besides, I didn't want to be the one who told her to go out there and face it.

And I didn't want to be the one responsible for what happened if she couldn't pull it off — if she went out there and could not hide her fear.

Would the *thing* be encouraged by that? Would it gain strength from her fear? Would the fingers reach even further and further up the boardwalk?

I didn't know. And I didn't want to find out.

Suddenly, the wind must have grown stronger than ever. It slammed hard against the front of the building, facing the boardwalk. The whole building shook.

Only a few of the lights in the ceiling were on. They were the ones I'd pushed the switches for when we first came in. They trembled when the wind struck so hard. The shadows they cast trembled, too, creating an eerie shimmering on the walls.

There were a lot of glasses and souvenir dishes in the glass counters. The dishes all said things like "Greetings from Seacoast City." They rattled.

Everything in the arcade shook and rattled. Including Mary and me.

The whole arcade was being hit by the strongest wind yet. Outside, it was screaming and howling like a pack of monsters or demons. I knew what it wanted.

It wanted us.

Or, at least, it wanted Mary.

I realized I was holding my breath, and had been for a long time. I let it out and looked at her.

She tried to smile, but it came out as some kind of terrible look of fear. She drew in a long, deep breath.

"I know what I have to do," she said. "I'll do it. I'll go outside."

I didn't know what to say. I just nodded.

"You did it, so I guess I can do it," she said.

She swallowed.

"Let's go," she said.

Chapter Twenty-Nine

We walked slowly to the door. It was still rattling and thumping as the wind banged against it.

"I'll come with you," I said.

"You don't have to," she said.

"I'll come with you," I repeated.

Mary didn't argue. She just nodded.

"Let's go," I said.

Once again, we got down on the floor. I pulled the door open and leaned against it while Mary crawled out beneath the steel shutter. I followed right behind her. I moved as quickly as I could.

Partly, I wanted to stay close to her. Partly, I wanted to do it and get outside before I had a chance to think about what I was doing. If I thought about it too much, I don't know if I would have been able to face that thing again.

We were outside, in the wind and the rain. The hurricane was worse than ever. The wind screamed in our ears. It took our breath away, and we both doubled over. It was deafening. Mary yelled something at me but I couldn't hear her.

Rain lashed at our faces, stinging our skin and making us close our eyes.

First, Mary's hood blew off her head. Then mine blew off. Our slickers were whipping and snapping around us.

I was blinded by the rain and deafened by the roaring of the wind. How could anything be left standing in a wind like that?

And then I heard it coming.

It seemed impossible that the roaring of the wind could get even louder, but it did.

It had to be the face in the wave, the . . . *thing*.

I forced my eyes open. I could hardly see through the sheets of rain that kept whipping at my eyes. But I saw it.

It was coming back.

Mary could hardly stand up in the wind. She

was fighting just to keep her balance. I reached out and took hold of her arm. That helped both of us to stand still.

The wave was gathering. Even through all the rain and spray in the air, I saw it growing and swelling as it rolled in from the ocean.

It just kept getting bigger and bigger. It was taller than the arcade. In another second, it was taller than our house.

It was a wall of water rushing toward the boardwalk. It was about to smash into it.

It looked so tall and terrible that I was sure it was going to get us. It would crash into the boardwalk and crush it into splinters!

And it would crush us, too. First, it would smash us into a bloody pulp. Then it would pick us up and whirl us around in the air like grains of sand. And then it would just throw us away, like all the other bits of broken junk it was whipping around in the air.

Two lampposts at the edge of the boardwalk, opposite the arcade, had been blown down. Another was still standing, swaying in the wind, its metal twisted.

The wave rushed forward. It towered high above the lamppost. When it struck, there'd be nothing left.

Rain hit me in the eyes. It felt like gravel that had been thrown in my face with terrific force. I snapped my head away.

I was still holding Mary's arm. I felt her arm stiffen. I forced my eyes open.

The wave was about to crest. White foam boiled at its top. I had to lean my head back to see all of it. And there it was again.

I saw that face.

The eyes flashed and glared at us. The mouth opened and the winds roared out of it.

The face was different now. The nose had turned into a snout, like that of a snarling dog. Saliva dribbled from its twisted lips. It had fangs. Its teeth snapped once, twice.

The thing threw its head back and howled at the skies.

And when it lowered its head, I knew it was looking right at Mary.

She stood her ground.

She was trembling violently — so was I — but we stayed there and faced it together.

The wave towered above us like an apartment building, and then it smashed itself down on the boardwalk. Even above the noise of the screaming wind, I could hear wooden boards being torn apart and metal being twisted like paper clips.

The boardwalk swayed beneath our feet. That must be what an earthquake feels like. The wave thundered all around us.

Spray from the crashing water struck us. It knocked us backwards, but we stayed on our feet.

Mary turned her head toward me. It was almost impossible to see. My eyes stung. There was salt water in them. It hurt to keep them open.

Mary was shouting something but I had no idea what she was saying. Then she turned and I knew she wanted to go back inside the arcade. So did I.

The wind nearly knocked us off our feet. We had to double over and fight against it. For a few seconds I didn't think we'd ever reach the door. It felt like our feet were walking forward but our bodies were being pushed backward.

I was afraid the wind was going to push us further and further away from the door, further and further from safety.

But we bent low to the ground and fought and clawed our way to the door. Finally, we dropped to our knees in front of it.

Mary crawled through and I followed right behind her.

Somehow, I got the door closed. I leaned back against it to keep it from banging. We were both pressing our fingers against our eyes. Salt water stings!

We were panting and struggling to catch our breath. All around us, everything in the arcade was shaking and rattling.

And then I suddenly became aware of a sound that was a thousand times worse than everything else we'd heard. It made me a thousand times more frightened than I already was.

Now I knew for sure that we had lost the battle.

I knew we were going to be killed and torn apart in a couple of seconds.

Chapter Thirty

Mary's head snapped around and she looked in the same direction I was looking. We crawled closer to each other.

That sound!

It was a banging sound, a thudding sound. We hadn't heard anything like it before. I knew where it was coming from.

The trap door!

The thing, the thing in the water, the thing in the wave, was underneath us.

It had gotten under the boardwalk and under the arcade. It was outside and all around us. And now it was underneath us too.

The monster was everywhere. The beast was in the waves and in the wind and the rain and the air.

Now the beast outside was also the beast beneath the boardwalk.

It was hammering and pounding at the underside of the trap door. How long could a little lock hold tight against that kind of force?

The floor trembled. The beast battered against the trap door, which jumped and popped in the middle of the floor. A terrible, screeching howl came from beneath our feet.

That was it. My mind went blank. There was nothing to do. We couldn't go outside, and now, with the beast beneath the boardwalk, we couldn't stay inside.

I counted the seconds till I died.

Chapter Thirty-One

Mary turned back to face me.

She said something but I couldn't hear her. The floor was shaking beneath us. The whole building was shaking and everything in it was rattling.

Somewhere near me, something fell over. I heard glass breaking.

Mary crawled up beside me. She put her mouth next to my ear.

" . . . me!" was all I heard.

I shouted as loud as I could. "What?"

"Help me!" she cried.

I opened my mouth and shrugged my shoulders. I couldn't think of anything to do. I couldn't help her and I couldn't help myself.

We were doomed. We were going to die.

"Help me!" Mary yelled into my ear again.

She was pointing back into the arcade, stabbing her finger frantically in the air. I couldn't figure out what she was pointing at. She pulled at my sleeve and then started crawling away.

I crawled after her.

The whole arcade was shivering and shaking. The arcade machines jumped and skipped in place. The pounding on the underside of the trap door sounded like a maniac was doing it.

Mary kept crawling, past the first few games and on toward the darker shadows. I thought she must have gone out of her mind. Fear had driven her crazy.

Then I saw she was standing up. The floor was shaking so violently that she had to pull herself upright against one of the games.

She held onto it until I reached her. I pulled myself up and stood beside her.

Mary was shaking her head, no. She was pointing at the floor.

I looked down. I didn't see anything.

Mary leaned against me.

"Plug it in!" she yelled next to my ear. "Plug it in! Hurry!"

Then she turned away and got herself around to the other side of the machine she was leaning against. She started pushing it.

At first, I didn't move because I didn't understand what she was doing. I thought she was just crazy. Terror had driven her stark raving mad, like car crash victims who wander around vaguely looking for their shoes.

She was worried that the machine was not plugged in? Did she want to play a couple of games to calm her nerves?

Then I didn't move because I was amazed. I saw what Mary was doing.

It might work!

It was nutty but it might just work.

Maybe.

Maybe.

I bent over and groped around for the electric cord.

Chapter Thirty-Two

The fortune-teller!

That hideous, cackling laugh that had scared us out of our minds when we first came into the arcade!

Mary wanted to turn it on so the machine would laugh at the wind!

I groped around on the floor behind it. My fingers were numb from the cold. I could barely feel anything. It was so dark, it was hard to see. I groped and felt, but I couldn't . . .

There! I had it!

I pulled the cord through my fingers until I found the plug. I dropped to my knees and swept my fingers across the floor until they struck the big socket.

I had it. I couldn't see the socket clearly. I tried to plug the machine in, but I couldn't get it right. I felt the socket with my fingers again, trying to feel which way the slots went without plugging my fingers in and electrocuting myself.

I had to jab the plug into the socket a couple of times before I got it into the right holes.

There! It went in!

Ha ha! Hee tree tree! Ha ha! Hee tree tree!

It was the most beautiful sound I'd ever heard in my life.

I stood up and began to help Mary. I saw that she was trying to turn the machine around so it faced the front door and the boardwalk.

And the ocean and the storm.

And the thing.

She gestured wildly toward the door. What did she want me to do? I couldn't understand.

Suddenly I knew.

This was the really risky part, but we had nothing to lose and everything to gain. We had our lives to gain!

The floor was jumping so badly I had to hold onto things to get there, but I finally reached the door.

I pulled it open and held it. The wind howled. Sheets of rain sliced by horizontally, blown so hard they were not falling from the sky to the ground, but whipping from one end of the boardwalk all the way to the other.

The wind sucked at my clothes. I felt I was going to be pulled out the door and tossed into the storm.

There was a doorstop attached to the outside of the glass. I pushed it down with the toe of my wet sneaker. It pressed against the door and held it open.

I looked back at Mary.

She was still struggling to turn the heavy machine around, grasping and heaving and hauling. She pointed and gestured toward the door. She made believe she was pushing something up.

Of course! The steel shutter!

I dropped down and crawled through the opening to get under the shutter. Salty spray stung my face and my eyes, but this time I didn't care. This time, I could stand anything.

I knew I could, because this time we were going to win.

Behind me, the witch kept up that horrible, cackling laugh.

Ha ha! Hee tree tree! Ha ha! Hee tree tree!

I pushed up against the shutter. It was heavy and it jammed for a second. Then it moved again. I gave a hard shove. The shutter rolled up.

Rain like a bucket of water hit me in the face. For a second, I couldn't see or breathe.

But the shutter was up and the door was open, and that laugh came screeching out of the arcade.

Ha ha! Hee tree tree! Ha ha! Hee tree tree!

Mary appeared in the doorway. The wind roared and hurled stinging rain and spray at us, but we stayed right where we were.

Behind us, the witch went right on laughing. No storm was going to stop her, and no wind was going to howl louder than she could.

Ha ha! Hee tree tree! Ha ha! Hee tree tree!

I couldn't help it. I started laughing. Beside me, Mary started laughing too.

I looked at her. As soon as our eyes met, we both started laughing even harder.

Ha ha! Hee tree tree! Ha ha! Hee tree tree!

And the harder we laughed, the harder we had to laugh. We laughed at the boardwalk, at the rain, at the wind. We laughed because the witch kept laughing.

Ha ha! Hee tree tree! Ha ha! Hee tree tree!

Then I realized that there was something I was not hearing. I was not hearing the pounding and hammering at the trap door.

It had stopped.

I turned an ear toward the doorway to be sure. There was no sound at all coming from the trap door. The only sound coming from the arcade now was the hysterical laughter of the witch.

Ha ha! Hee tree tree! Ha ha! Hee tree tree!

I turned back toward the ocean.

I was expecting to see the wave, and there it was. It was just like before, green and gray and white, boiling up as it raced toward the boardwalk. White foam frothed at the top where it began to curl forward.

Mary and I had both stopped laughing.

No! We couldn't stop laughing! Not now!

I forced myself to laugh. A big, loud laughing sound came out of my mouth. It didn't sound very funny. But it was a laugh. And that was what mattered.

I gestured at Mary. She caught on right away. She started laughing with me.

The wave towered above us. It was about to crest and come crashing down.

And I saw that face again.

I couldn't tell if it was some horribly deformed human face or the face of some sick, mad animal.

It howled and howled. The wind from it nearly knocked us off our feet.

But we stood there and faced it.

Now I knew it couldn't beat us.

The eyes flashed and the fangs dripped and it howled and howled.

But now it was different. It didn't sound the way it had before. It wasn't as loud. And it wasn't as frightening.

For a second that seemed to last for minutes, the huge wave hung in the air above the boardwalk.

The face tossed right and left. The eyes flew in every direction, as if they were searching for something.

I knew that, now, they would find nothing.

With a groan of pain, the wave crested and toppled forward toward the boardwalk. The face, twisted in pain and hate and fury, broke up into a thousand streams of water and disappeared.

When the wave fell onto the boardwalk, it had lost its strength. It just collapsed there.

And from that second, the wind began to die away a little. The rain became slightly less heavy. And the dark sky grew just a little bit lighter.

The whole world around us became just a little bit quieter.

Now there was just a strong wind and a heavy rain instead of a howling storm.

Little by little, Mary and I let our fake laughter fade away too.

And finally the loudest sound in our world was the laughter of the witch inside the arcade.

She just went on and on, laughing and

laughing at the hideous forces that had threatened us and almost killed us.

Almost.

Ha ha! Hee tree tree! Ha ha! Hee tree tree!

Chapter Thirty-Three

When the storm was over and things got back to normal, Mary and I had a lot of explaining to do.

It wasn't easy.

Basically, we told my parents what had happened.

Basically.

There was a lot of damage in Seacoast City and on the boardwalk, but nobody was killed.

My parents had been stuck for a long time on the other side of the bridge. When the storm got so bad so fast, the police had closed the bridge so cars wouldn't be blown off it.

Wise move.

Mary and I had fun for the rest of that month. We both helped out Uncle Louie in the arcade.

And we both fed a lot of Uncle Louie's

quarters into that fortune-telling machine. Uncle Louie thought we were nuts.

We didn't care.

Every time you put a quarter in it, a little card with a fortune printed on it comes out of a slot. Mary and I never even looked at them.

We just wanted to hear that witch laughing. Other people hated it, but we thought it was the best sound in the world.

LET, LET, LET THE MAILMAN GIVE YOU COLD, CLAMMY *SHIVERS! SHIVERS! SHIVERS!!!*

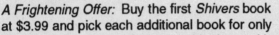

A Frightening Offer: Buy the first *Shivers* book at $3.99 and pick each additional book for only $1.99. Please include $2.00 for shipping and handling. Canadian orders: Please add $1.00 per book. (Allow 4-6 weeks for delivery.)